DISCARD

796.357 Johnson, Rick L
Joh
     Jim Abbott

DATE DUE

796.357   Johnson, Rick L

JOH   JIM ABBOTT

DATE DUE	BORROWER'S NAME	ROOM NUMBER
9-7-9_	Chris	20
	Richard	19
	Trey	2

JIM ABBOTT

JIM ABBOTT
Beating the Odds

by Rick L. Johnson

DILLON PRESS, INC.
Minneapolis, Minnesota 55415

Photographic Acknowledgments

The photographs are reproduced through the courtesy of the Amateur Athletic Union; the California Angels; Flint Central High school; *The Journal*, David Larzelere, Librarian; Bob Kalmbach, University of Michigan Information Services; the University of Michigan.

Library of Congress Cataloging-in-Publication Data

Johnson, Rich L.
    Jim Abbott : beating the odds / Rick L. Johnson.
       p. cm. — (Taking part books)
    Includes bibliographical references and index.
    Summary: A biography of the one-handed pitcher of the California Angels baseball team.
    ISBN 0-87518-484-7
    1. Abbott, Jim, 1967- —Juvenile literature. 2. Baseball players—United States—Biography—Juvenile literature. 3. Pitchers (Baseball)—United States—Biography—Juvenile literature.
[1. Abbott, Jim, 1967- . 2. Baseball players.] I. Title.
GV865.A26J64   1991
796.357' 092—dc20
[B]
                               91-7561
                                 CIP
                                 AC

Dillon Press, Inc., 242 Portland Avenue South
Minneapolis, Minnesota 55415

Printed in the United States of America
1 2 3 4 5 6 7 8 9 10 99 98 97 96 95 94 93 92 91

CONTENTS

JIM ABBOTT

Jim Abbott's long list of baseball achievements include at least two that few other players can claim.

In 1987 Abbott starred for both the University of Michigan and the United States national team. After a season of outstanding pitching, he became the first baseball player ever to win the Sullivan Award. That high honor is presented each year to the nation's best amateur athlete.

In 1989, skipping the minor leagues, Abbott won 12 games for the California Angels. Since 1965, no player going directly from amateur baseball to the major leagues had won more than 6 games.

Those who haven't seen Abbott pitch may ask how someone born without a right hand manages to play baseball. His pitching delivery, though, is quite natural. Fans soon begin to notice his blazing fastball and smooth fielding.

But there is more to Jim Abbott's story than his sudden success as a major league baseball pitcher. It began with parents who encouraged him to make his own decisions and "let him dream of anything." It continued with his first no-hit game, a hard-hitting high school football showdown, and a tense Olympic battle for the gold medal. And it reached a peak with a thrilling victory during Abbott's first major league season.

 # THEY LET HIM DREAM

Mike and Kathy Abbott saw the pain of five-year-old Jim spilling over into tears as their son entered the house and blurted out his story. The other children, he cried, wouldn't let him play with them.

Jim was feeling the hurt of being left out. At some point most children are told they are too little, or they talk different, or some other wounding remark. To Jim, they had said he couldn't join their game because he had only one hand.

Mike and Kathy Abbott shared their son's pain. The easiest action for either of them to take would have been to let their little boy crawl into their lap and remain there. Perhaps the hardest was what they did.

"We love you, son, but you can't come in here

looking for sympathy," Mike Abbott told Jim. "You have to handle this yourself."

His parents turned him around and sent him outdoors again. To some people, that may have seemed cruel. But Mike and Kathy Abbott had always treated Jim like any other child. They weren't going to allow his disability, or handicap, to prevent him from having a normal childhood.

Today, Jim speaks with great respect for his mother and father. They were both only 18 years old when Jim was born in Flint, Michigan, on September 19, 1967.

"When I was little my parents always encouraged me to be outgoing," Jim remembers. "My dad was always pushing me, when I'd see someone new, to walk up to the kid, shake his hand and say, 'Hi, my name is Jim Abbott.' He really encouraged that."

Some of the decisions his parents had to make

were not easy ones. They fitted him with an artificial hand—one with clamping metal hooks—when he was about four years old. Jim hated wearing it. For one thing, its harsh look seemed to frighten other children. Finally, after about a year, they decided to let him quit wearing it.

But the happy times during Jim's childhood far outweighed any unpleasant moments. He has fond memories of family trips, fishing, and tossing a football with his dad.

Jim also played soccer and basketball, but baseball was his favorite sport. When he wasn't playing on an organized team or in neighborhood games, he was throwing a ball against a wall near his home in Flint.

"Like every other kid, I pictured myself as Nolan Ryan, or whoever," remembers Jim. "I just threw the ball against the wall and played those imaginary games."

No one told him that a boy with one hand should not be imagining himself in the major leagues. Instead, as *Time* magazine reported, "They let him dream of anything."

Jim's natural ability impressed his family, friends, and teammates. In his first midget league baseball game, he pitched a five-inning no-hitter. "It surprised me quite a bit," Jim later recalled. "You know, though, I walked 11, too, so...."

In addition to talent, Jim gained respect for the speed of his now well-known glove transfer. Even then, it earned praise from coaches and fans.

"I was amazed he could play, let alone pitch," remembered Jeff Blanchard, one of Jim's first coaches. "He worked harder than anyone I've ever seen."

His hometown newspaper, the *Flint Journal*, featured Jim when he was nearly 12 years old and playing for Blanchard's team. In mid-July that summer, he had a 6-0 record and had struck out 74 batters in just 32 innings. Jim had an earned-run average of 0.00.* In other words, he had not allowed a single earned run. He was also batting .562.

Flint sportswriter Chuck Johnson asked Jim what his parents thought of him playing baseball. "They don't want me to get big-headed," he replied.

Like other young players, Jim became excited when he was asked about his favorite major league athletes. He liked them all.

"I look at them and wish it was me," Jim said.

And no one in Flint was telling him it couldn't be.

Earned run average is the average number of earned runs a pitcher allows in nine innings.

Chapter 2

THAT GREAT ABBOTT SWITCH

During a freshman baseball game at Flint Central High School, Mike Abbott talked with varsity baseball coach Bob Holec. His son worked on the mound.

Varsity players will be stronger and faster, the coach warned, and fielding might be a problem. As the game continued, Holec discussed Jim's chances of playing for the Flint Central team.

Mike Abbott watched Jim take his stretch and glance at the runner on first base. Suddenly, a hard one-hopper rocketed toward the mound. Jim caught the ball and quickly fired to second base to begin a double play. Mike Abbott spoke to the coach about his son. "Well," he noted, "I guess he can handle grounders back at him."

Jim Abbott in his high school baseball uniform.

Mike Abbott knew, though, that Holec had given him an honest view of Jim's future as a baseball player. He shared some of the same concerns. "With every step, we thought about whether it would catch up to him," said Mike Abbott. Jim's father feared that at some level, perhaps in high school, the ability of other athletes could end his success.

But Jim continued to star at Flint Central. Helping to make that possible was what reporters would later call "That Great Abbott Switch." Jim had learned his rapid glove transfer during those hours of throwing a ball against the wall near his home.

At first, Flint Central fans watched his pitching method with amazement. Jim began his windup with his glove resting on the end of his right arm. The mitt remained balanced there as he delivered the pitch. His motion was as fluid and natural as any left-hander. As the ball neared home plate, Jim slipped

During a Flint Central game, Jim Abbott fields a hard-hit ball after switching his glove to his pitching hand.

his pitching hand into his glove, preparing to field the ball.

After he caught a ball thrown or hit to him, he quickly switched the glove back to his right arm. He then grabbed the ball with his left hand. That way he was ready to throw again.

Some teams thought it might be easier to bunt or to steal home against Jim than against other pitchers. But his glove transfers were so fast that their attempts usually failed.

As a sophomore Jim posted a 6-4 record and made Flint's all-city team. As a junior he was 8-3, again made the all-city team, and played on the all-Saginaw Valley team.

Jim's summer job also involved baseball. He worked for Flint's parks and recreation board, coaching 8- to 13-year-olds. Even then, many of these young players admired him enough to ask for his autograph.

Jim Abbott cheers for his teammates from the bench during a high school game.

During the summer, Jim also played on a Connie Mack League baseball team. His friendly, outgoing manner made him popular with his teammates. During his final year, they chose him to be a team captain.

One of Jim's greatest high school athletic

As the Flint Central quarterback, Jim Abbott hands off the ball to a running back.

experiences came on the football field. Baseball coach Bob Holec had urged him to try the sport his junior year. He thought that Jim would enjoy the strong team spirit on a football squad. During his first season, Jim served as a back-up quarterback. He started some games in his senior year.

One of his starting assignments was in a quarterfinal state playoff contest against Midland. He threw one touchdown pass early in the game. Then, in the second quarter, he dropped back deep in his own territory to pass on third down. Just after Jim released the ball, a lineman plowed into his midsection. Jim rolled to the ground. As he reached toward the pain in his right arm, he spotted his wide receiver clutching the pass.

The play gained 34 yards. But Flint Central fans in the crowd grew quiet as Jim's injury forced him to walk slowly off the field. "There's not a kid in school who doesn't like Jim Abbott," assistant football coach Sam Paraschos said after the game. "He's just a nice kid."

Only one play later, the crowd roared with excitement as the strong-armed quarterback trotted toward Central's huddle. "The kid is talented but the thing he's really got is guts," commented head football coach Jim Eufinger.

Back on the field, Jim's athletic ability took center stage. He finished the game with four touchdown passes, leading Central to an exciting 26-20 victory.

After the game, instead of his own performance, Jim talked about the outstanding routes his receivers ran. He also mentioned the support he had received from his family while playing for Flint Central.

Since Jim had entered high school, Kathy Abbott had returned to law school and was now starting a new career. Mike Abbott kept busy as a sales manager. Having them find time to be in the stands for his games meant a lot to him.

Also cheering for Jim was his brother Chad, four years younger than him. "He takes a lot of stuff about following in his brother's footsteps, but he works hard in school," Jim said of the other child in the

Abbott family. "He's an excellent soccer player."

Despite his success in football, Jim knew his future was in baseball. His senior year record showed why the University of Michigan wanted him for a starting pitcher. During his final season for Flint Central, Jim had a 10-3 record and pitched three no-hitters. He struck out more than two batters per inning and earned all-state honors.

At the plate, gripping his right wrist and the bat with his left hand, his achievements were equally remarkable. He batted .427 and led the team in home runs with seven. When Jim was not pitching, he played first base. As Flint's clean-up hitter, he had five late-inning, game-winning hits.

Natural ability was one reason for Jim's success. But coaches also gave other reasons. His willingness to listen to instruction and advice, and his hard work throughout the year, even during the off-season, were

In high school, Jim Abbott worked hard to increase his strength and skills as a baseball player.

both important. A weight-training program increased his upper-body strength. "And he's a competitor," added coach Holec. "He wants to beat you."

One of Jim's most disappointing losses came in the final game of his high school career. In the championship of a tournament involving more than

30 teams from the Flint area, Central lost to Flushing, 1-0. Jim had not allowed a run until the bottom of the ninth inning.

After the game, and after his teammates had left, Jim sat alone in the dugout. He was still thinking about the loss. Flint Central's athletic director, Tim Bograkos, saw the tears in Jim's eyes as he walked toward him.

"Go ahead, kid, have a cry," Bograkos said, sitting down beside him. "You deserve it. But let me tell you something, young man. Your days as a baseball player are not through. I don't know how far your ability is going to take you, but I can tell you one thing. You've been a credit to our team, to our city, and to your family, and for that you should be extremely proud."

Now Bograkos's eyes grew moist, too. He knew that Flint Central was going to miss this young man.

Chapter 3

LAYOVERS IN NEW DELHI

A low rumbling from the gathering crowd drifted across the University of Michigan's Ray Fisher Stadium. The starting pitcher for the 1986 home opener would be first-year Wolverine Jim Abbott.

Michigan had a national reputation as a football powerhouse, but the school was used to winning in other sports, too. Today, many in the crowd wondered about the freshman going to the mound.

Abbott had been a high school star, but could he compete at a major university? How well could he field? Was he as good an athlete as the newspaper articles claimed?

Within three innings against Grand Valley State College, Jim answered all the questions. Not only did

University of Michigan fans soon recognized Jim Abbott as a new star pitcher for their college team.

he pitch hitless baseball, he turned in two outstanding fielding plays. Once he hustled behind the mound to pull down a high-chopping ground ball and throw out the sprinting runner.

Now the crowd buzzed with excitement. During recent years they had watched stars such as Rick Leach, Chris Sabo, and Barry Larkin perform for the Wolverines. The University of Michigan fans knew how to recognize baseball talent. They decided that this young left-hander was going to fit in well on their team.

During his freshman year, Abbott posted a 6-2 record for the Wolverines. In the Big Ten tournament championship that year, he entered the game in the third inning. At that point Michigan trailed Minnesota 4-3. Jim didn't allow a hit until the eighth inning, and Michigan rallied for a 9-5 win.

Abbott's record improved to 11-3 during his

Jim Abbott's pitching skills sometimes made opposing batters appear almost helpless.

sophomore year. Between April 4 and May 6, he pitched 35 innings without allowing an earned run. The outstanding streak started against UCLA in the Metrodome in Minneapolis, and it included shutouts against Purdue and Ohio State.

Jim's talents sometimes made college hitters appear

almost helpless. "Batters didn't want to be hitting against him when he was throwing hard," said Jim Schneider of the Michigan Sports Information Department. "On days he was getting his breaking ball over, it was really unfair because he could just play with them."

The streak had reached 31 straight scoreless innings when Indiana scored an unearned run against Abbott.* For the whole college season, he had a 2.08 earned run average.

That summer, in Millington, Tennessee, Jim tried out for the United States national team. As expected, he earned a position as a starting pitcher for Team USA. This group of amateur players represents the United States in games against other nations.

On the 1987 Team USA tour, Abbott finished with an excellent 8-1 record and a 1.70 earned run average. In Indianapolis he helped the United States

*An unearned run is one that scores because of a team's fielding error.

win a silver medal at the Pan American games.

With those types of performances, Abbott began to earn high honors. He received the 1987 Golden Spikes Award, presented each year to the nation's outstanding amateur baseball player.

As the Golden Spikes winner, he became a candidate for the Sullivan Award. That great honor goes to the country's top amateur athlete.

No baseball player had ever won the award. Jim Abbott went to the March 1988 dinner expecting his biggest honor to be meeting the other nominees. Those included track and field athletes Jackie Joyner-Kersee and Greg Foster, diver Greg Louganis, and basketball player David Robinson.

"When they announced his name, his eyes grew nine miles wide," said a member of the audience. But no one else was as surprised as Jim Abbott. People who followed sports knew that, both on and off the

Holding the trophy high, Jim Abbott accepts the Sullivan Award as the best amateur athlete in the United States.

field, no athlete could better represent amateur athletics.

Jim had been a good student in high school. In college his grades remained above average despite his busy schedule. Abbott's major field of study was communications, which prepares students for careers such as television broadcasting.

His sense of humor helped make him popular with other students. Accepting the Sullivan Award, Jim joked that he had just given his teacher a note so that he could miss speech class. Now, because he won the award, he had to give a speech after all.

Abbott's outstanding amateur play continued in the summer of 1988. That year Team USA traveled from Italy to Japan to the Summer Olympic Games in Seoul, South Korea. On the tour Jim led the way with an 8-1 record and a 2.55 earned run average. "Playing against the world's best amateur teams was a real confidence builder for me as a pitcher," he said.

The Olympic team was on the road from June 10 through the end of September. Abbott knew that few baseball teams had a more demanding schedule. He doubted that even minor league bus rides could compare to the demands of this trip. "In the minors," he joked, "they don't have any layovers in New Delhi, India."

The most exciting Team USA game was the Olympic gold medal contest in Seoul on September 28. Jim Abbott pitched against Japanese ace Takehiro Ishii. He allowed a second-inning run that gave Japan a 1-0 advantage.

In the fourth inning, the United States took the lead when Tino Martinez smashed a two-run homer over the center field fence. Team USA added a run in the fourth and the fifth to go in front 4-1.

Japan threatened to regain the lead in the bottom

While he attended the University of Michigan, Jim Abbott represented his country on Team USA at the 1988 Summer Olympic Games in Seoul, South Korea.

of the sixth. Two hits and a walk suddenly loaded the bases against Abbott. Then he walked another batter to force home Japan's second run.

Perhaps 1988 was going to be a repeat of the last Olympics. In 1984, Japan defeated the United States in the Olympic finals in Los Angeles.

Team USA coach Mark Marquess considered

switching pitchers, but decided to stick with his ace. His decision proved to be the right one. One more run scored on a routine ground ball. But Jim rediscovered his control and escaped the sixth with the United States clinging to a 4-3 lead. With Abbott again firing strike after strike, the United States carried a 5-3 lead into the bottom of the ninth inning.

It had been 14 years since a United States baseball team had won a gold medal in a major international competition. Now the players were only three outs away from winning the Olympic title.

The first two batters grounded out to Team USA's talented third baseman, Robin Ventura. Jim Abbott took a deep breath. He went into his windup and hurled the pitch. Another grounder rolled toward third base. Ventura fielded the ball and threw to Martinez at first base for the final out.

Jim leaped into the air, arms thrust high in

triumph. He raced toward first base to hug Tino Martinez. The two Olympic heroes soon found themselves mobbed by celebrating teammates.

Many Olympic champions were superb solo performers. The glory was theirs alone as they stood on the victory stand. But winning a gold medal in a team sport had its advantages. It meant a lot to be able to hug a teammate. Jim Abbott would never forget sharing the triumph with the friends he had worked so hard with all summer.

Jim laughed as he looked across at teammate Mike Fiore planting an American flag on the pitcher's mound. The impressive records he had set at Michigan could not equal this victory. All of the trophies he had received could not create this feeling. In fact, nothing he had accomplished in sports could match the thrill of Olympic gold.

Chapter 4

WATCH WHAT HE CAN DO

Jim Abbott hurled a fastball through the desert wind. A white blur zoomed past the batter, veteran major league infielder Tim Flannery. Thrown at a blazing 94 miles per hour, even the catcher couldn't hold on to the explosive pitch.

Flannery finally managed to ground out to first base. Abbott's first inning as a professional was complete. He had struck out two San Diego Padres and not allowed a single hit.

Surrounded by the constant clicking of cameras, Jim took a quick look around the spring training stadium in Yuma, Arizona. He was not a Little Leaguer dreaming. He really was pitching in a big-league uniform—for now, at least. The California

During 1989 spring training, Jim Abbott soon proved that he belonged in a big-league uniform.

Angels said he would start the 1989 regular season in the minor leagues. Few players went from college directly to the major leagues, even first-round draft picks such as Abbott. All he could do, he decided, was to try to pitch his best during the exhibition season.

Coaches and teammates were already impressed with his actions off the baseball diamond. Jim fielded questions about his disability as smoothly as he worked on the mound. When asked to give his advice to disabled children, his answer was a simple one many would remember: "Don't let it get you down."

The crowd of reporters, photographers, and camera crews would have bothered even many seasoned veterans. Abbott, though, kept his mind focused on his goal of playing for the Angels. But he also knew that the interviews were important to young people with disabilities. "If the story helps out someone with a problem, then it makes what I'm doing all the more worthwhile," he once said.

Still, there were times when it wasn't easy. One reporter thoughtlessly asked Jim if anyone else in his family was "deformed." Abbott replied politely and patiently to such questions. "He's had to answer some of the dumbest, most undignified questions I've ever heard," said California manager Doug Rader, "but he's handled everything with dignity and grace."

Teammates quickly accepted Jim as "one of the guys." When bull pen catcher Rick Turner was told he would be Abbott's roommate, he wondered if he might need to assist him with some routine tasks. He soon learned that would not be necessary. "You don't ask him what he can't do," said Turner. "Just sit back and watch what he can do."

On the field, Jim impressed everyone in the Angels camp. Longtime major league catcher Lance Parrish had this to say about the rookie pitcher. "He probably has as strong an arm as any left-hander I've caught. His motion is so fluid, the ball just kind of explodes."

Abbott also knew how to move his fastball inside and outside, and up and down in the strike zone. That surprised many major league scouts. They weren't used to seeing a 21-year-old with that kind of knowledge of the art of pitching.

All spring Jim worked hard to improve his curve ball and his ability to hold runners on base. Meanwhile, he won two games while losing only one. His pitching skills forced the California Angels to make a difficult decision. Should they change their plans for him to gain experience in the minor leagues?

Since 1965, only nine pitchers had skipped minor league baseball and moved directly into the major leagues. None had completed their first big-league season with more than six wins. Only one—

Going directly from college baseball to the major leagues was a difficult step to make. Few pitchers in modern baseball history had done it successfully.

Burt Hooton, 2-0, 1971—had avoided a losing record.

The Angels knew that moving directly to the major leagues would be hard for Abbott. But they also knew that they needed his fastball in their starting rotation. The Angels decided to place Jim's name on the major league roster. His first pitching assignment would come on April 8 against the Seattle Mariners.

Abbott's opening game was one of the most widely watched in baseball history. As he moved toward the bull pen to warm up, he was surrounded by a dozen television camera operators and two dozen photographers.

At the start of the first inning, the Anaheim Stadium crowd roared its encouragement. Abbott prepared to face Harold Reynolds, the Seattle leadoff batter. Reynolds grounded a hit between first and second. Then Henry Cotto followed with a line-drive single. Both runners scored in the inning, giving

The California Angels play their home games at Anaheim Stadium in Orange County in southern California.

Mariner pitcher Mark Langston a 2-0 lead. "There was definitely some nervousness there," Jim said. "Maybe I wasn't as clearly focused as I should have been."

For once, all of the reporters and photographers seemed to bother Abbott. In the past, he had appeared on "Good Morning America" and "Donahue." He had been featured in *Sports Illustrated* and *Sport*. He had been covered by *USA Today* and many other newspapers. But on this night, there was a flood of attention greater than any he had ever experienced.

Abbott struggled into the fifth inning before manager Doug Rader was forced to remove him. In nearly five innings, he allowed six hits and six runs, three of them earned. He walked three batters. "I really didn't have my good stuff," Jim said after California's 7-0 loss. "I think I was a bit unnerved by the attention, and it's nice to have that out of the way."

During his rookie season with the California Angels, Jim Abbott had to face constant pressures both on and off the field.

Five days later, Abbott took the mound against the powerful Oakland As. His pitching improved in the second game. Jim held Oakland scoreless from the second through the fifth innings. He also recorded his first major league strikeout against slugger Dave Parker.

But there were problems, too. Dave Henderson's first inning home run provided the As with an early 1-0 lead. In the second inning, Carney Lansford's sharp grounder reached the mound before Abbott completed his glove transfer. He knocked the ball down, but his hurried throw to first sailed high for his first major league error. Then in the sixth, Jim's final inning of the night, the As widened their lead to 4-0.

Abbott tried to remain positive after his second straight loss. "I'm feeling more confident in myself, more and more confident in being here," he told reporters.

Jim knew, though, that he had yet to prove himself as a major league pitcher. During his climb up the baseball ladder, people had often asked him if he could play at the next level. It was a pointless question, he thought, because his answer didn't really matter. What counted was how he performed on the field.

And on a major league diamond, Jim Abbott was still a young rookie trying to prove he belonged.

Chapter 5

FEEL SORRY FOR THE BATTERS

The mid-May game in Anaheim Stadium featured superstar pitcher Roger Clemens versus Jim Abbott. All of the statistics favored a Boston Red Sox win.

Clemens was a two-time Cy Young Award winner. Each year the best pitcher in the American League and the best pitcher in the National League win that award. This season Clemens had an excellent 5-1 record.

Abbott's record was only 2-3. He had earned his first major league win on April 24. In that game he hurled six innings in a 3-2 California victory against Baltimore. Now, on this Wednesday night, the odds were against another Abbott win.

Then the unexpected happened. The Angels

In May 1989, Jim Abbott defeated the Boston Red Sox and superstar Roger Clemens.

scored five runs against Clemens in the first inning. Abbott knew, though, that the game was far from over. He still had to face the hard-hitting Red Sox lineup that included Wade Boggs, Ellis Burks, and Mike Greenwell.

But the Angels pitcher did stop the Red Sox hitters. In fact, he pitched a complete game shutout and allowed only four singles. As *Newsweek* later reported, fans could only "feel sorry for the batters." Now they could cheer for their new pitcher. Welcome to the major leagues, Jim Abbott!

The Angels rookie continued to pitch well. As the season passed, more and more people became aware of his story. When Jim returned from road trips, the team's publicity staff rolled his mail to him in a shopping cart.

Abbott finished his first year with a 12-12 record and a 3.92 earned run average. His performances earned him a place on the Topps's All-Star rookie team.

The on-the-field challenges were not the only ones Abbott faced in his first year. Fans in each American League city looked forward to seeing him pitch. But they also wanted to read about him. As the Angels traveled to New York, Boston, and on around the league, he had to answer the never-ending questions of reporters.

There were times, Jim confessed to Mike Penner of the *Los Angeles Times*, when he badly wanted those tiresome questions to end. Like any person, he just wanted to think of himself as normal and be treated as such.

Gradually, though, he began to understand an important fact. Although playing baseball with one hand was different, that did not mean he was lacking in something necessary. "It's not a negative, it hasn't hindered me," he said. "It's just changed a few things."

To relax from the pressures of major league baseball, Jim enjoys playing golf with friends. He has had some of these friends since the fourth grade. Others are teammates and professional athletes from the Los Angeles area.

Jim lives in a condominium in Irvine, California. Irvine is not far from Anaheim. Both cities are in Orange County, south of Los Angeles. Like many young adults, Jim enjoys trips to the beach and to the movies. But baseball takes most of his time during the season. Jim is not married. In the winter, he often visits his family in Michigan.

By his second major league season, in 1990, the story of the hurdles Jim Abbott had overcome were well known. Then, writers and announcers began to pay more attention to Abbott's pitching performances.

During Jim Abbott's second season, attention focused on his pitching performance.

Jim Abbott has set an outstanding example for all young people to follow.

That was fine with Jim. He wanted to be viewed more as a baseball player than as a role model.

Today, the nation's baseball fans are learning what those who know him quickly realize. Jim Abbott is much more than simply an inspiring story about an athlete who has overcome difficult odds. He is a likable young man with a wide variety of outstanding qualities.

Years before, the coaches at Flint Central had learned that. They saw the tall, slender athlete standing above them, his eyes intense with a desire to follow their instructions. He worked hard to meet the goals they had set.

Later, his Olympic teammates had learned that. They saw Jim, even though he was often the center of attention, always trying to keep the team's interests first. He constantly pointed out other players' key hits or outstanding fielding plays.

And, in 1989, California Angels fans had learned that. They saw the quietly confident 21-year-old rookie firing fastballs across the inside corner of the plate. His pitching helped California challenge the Oakland As for the American League Western Division title.

Jim Abbott's life is filled with lessons for other young people. They are lessons about dreaming, about setting goals that may appear unreachable. They are also lessons about how to treat others, about giving them a chance to be friends or teammates.

But at the ball park, fans are more likely to be enjoying an exciting Abbott pitching performance.

They know all of his past achievements. And, sitting on the edge of their seats, they are ready to cheer all of his future victories.

JIM ABBOTT'S BASEBALL STATISTICS

For the University of Michigan

Year	G	IP	W	L	R	ER	SO	BB	GS	CG	SHO	SV	ERA
1986	14	50.1	6	2	34	23	44	34	10	1	1	0	4.11
1987	15	86.1	11	3	24	20	60	39	15	4	3	0	2.08
1988	17	97.2	9	3	54	36	82	56	16	8	2	0	3.32

For the California Angels

Year	G	IP	W	L	R	ER	SO	BB	GS	CG	SHO	SV	ERA
1989	29	181.1	12	12	95	79	115	74	29	4	2	0	3.92
1990	33	211.2	10	14	116	106	105	72	33	4	1	0	4.51

G–Games pitched
IP–Innings pitched
W–Wins
L–Losses
R–Runs allowed
ER–Earned runs allowed
SO–Strikeouts

BB–Bases on balls
GS–Games started
CG–Complete games
SHO–Shutouts
SV–Saves
ERA–Earned Run Average

AWARDS AND HONORS

1985   Signed baseball scholarship with the University of Michigan

1985   Named March of Dimes Athlete of the Year

1987   Named Philadelphia Sportswriters Association Most Courageous Athlete

1987   Received Golden Spikes Award from United States Baseball Federation

1987   Carried American flag in opening ceremonies of Pan American Games

1988   Named Big Ten Jesse Owens Male Athlete of the Year

1988   Named member of the *Sporting News* All-America College Baseball Team

1988   Won Sullivan Award from Amateur Athletic Union

1988   Received Tangueray Amateur Achievement Award

1988   Selected by U.S. Olympic Committee as "Athlete of the Year" for baseball

1988   Chosen in the first round (eighth pick overall) of major league baseball draft by California Angels

1989   Named to Topps's All-Star Rookie Team

INDEX

About the Author

Rick Johnson is a free-lance writer whose articles and short stories have appeared in a variety of publications. He has coached 8- to 12-year-old baseball players, including one who had a disability similar to Jim Abbott's. During his research for this book, the author interviewed Jim Abbott as well as several of his former coaches.

Mr. Johnson has won first place for column writing and first place for sports pages in the Kansas Press Association Better Newspaper Contest. A graduate of the University of Kansas School of Journalism, he and his wife live in Concordia, Kansas.

Milpitas Unified School District
Milpitas, California
Weller School